SIX KIDS

and a

STUFFED CAT

Also by Gary Paulsen

SIX KIDS

and a

STUFFED CAT

GARY PAULSEN

Simon & Schuster Books for Young Readers
New York   London   Toronto   Sydney   New Delhi

SIMON & SCHUSTER BOOKS FOR YOUNG READERS
An imprint of Simon & Schuster Children's Publishing Division
1230 Avenue of the Americas, New York, New York 10020

SIMON & SCHUSTER BOOKS FOR YOUNG READERS is a trademark of Simon & Schuster, Inc.
For information about special discounts for bulk purchases, please contact Simon & Schuster Special Sales at 1-866-506-1949 or business@simonandschuster.com.
The Simon & Schuster Speakers Bureau can bring authors to your live event. For more information or to book an event, contact the Simon & Schuster Speakers Bureau at 1-866-248-3049 or visit our website at www.simonspeakers.com.
Jacket design by Krista Vossen
Interior design Hilary Zarycky
The text for this book is set in ITC New Baskerville.
Manufactured in the United States of America
0416 FFG
2 4 6 8 10 9 7 5 3 1
Library of Congress Cataloging-in-Publication Data
Names: Paulsen, Gary.
Title: Six kids and a stuffed cat / Gary Paulsen.
Description: First edition. | New York : Simon & Schuster Books for Young Readers, [2016] | Summary: Six misfits get stuck together in a middle school restroom and discover friendship. Includes playscript of the story.
Identifiers: LCCN 2015026692| ISBN 9781481452236 (hardback) | ISBN 9781481452243 (paperback) | ISBN 9781481452250 (ebook)
Subjects: | CYAC: Middle schools—Fiction. | Schools—Fiction. | Friendship—Fiction. | Humorous stories. | BISAC: JUVENILE FICTION / Humorous Stories. | JUVENILE FICTION / Social Issues / Friendship. | JUVENILE FICTION / Animals / Cats.
Classification: LCC PZ7.P2843 Si 2016 | DDC [Fic]—dc23
LC record available at http://lccn.loc.gov/2015026692

FIRST
EDITION

This book is dedicated in memory of

George Nicholson.

He fought for my books.

And I am forever grateful.

Scene One:

"Don't step in the blood."

I was cramming tissue up both of my nostrils to stem the flow of my most recent nosebleed when a kid tried to sneak in the second-floor restroom at RJ Glavine Middle School without being noticed. Weird since it was a small space, full of mirrors, and I was Right There. The sink area of any bathroom is a hard place to pretend to be invisible.

And we were going to be stuck together for a while. Because this school is insanely paranoid whenever there's the tiniest threat of a storm. A couple minutes ago, I'd heard the overly cautious announcement warning everyone still on school property after school hours to huddle up and hunker down so the district couldn't get sued in case anything bad happened. That's not exactly what they said, but that's what I heard.

"Attention! A severe weather alert is likely to be issued for the surrounding areas. In the interest of erring on the side of caution and adhering to the guidelines of our prudent insurance liability policy, we strongly recommend that any faculty, staff, and students remaining in the school building immediately seek shelter in the nearest interior room. I repeat: Due to the slight possibility of potentially sudden onset heavy rain, please move immediately to a safe location, away from windows, and remain there until the all-clear sounds. Thank you."

Good thing I was already in one of the safest rooms in the building, dealing with what can only be described as rivers of blood coursing down my philtrum. That's the midline groove in the upper lip that runs from the top of the lip to the nose. I know that word because the one on my face is frequently bloody, so it seemed only right to learn its proper name. I'm a very impressive bleeder. And today, I'd left a small trail of blood in the second-floor bathroom at RJ Glavine Middle School and freaked out the new kid, also taking shelter from the—take my word on this—nonthreatening baby storm that was going to miss us by a mile.

"What?" The kid practically climbed the walls trying to dodge the blood after I pointed it out.

"You were about to walk right though the splatter. It's not nearly enough to be a puddle, but it's more than a sprinkle."

I adjusted the tissues I'd jammed up my bloody nose, hoping this kid thought bloody noses made a person seem a little mad, bad, and dangerous to know. I usually aim for being thought of as The Funny One because I'm, you know, inherently amusing. Plus, I overcompensate with humor to distract from the fact that I'm not really a people person.

Lately, though, I've been starting to feel my sarcastic take on things has been misunderstood and underappreciated. I thought it might be an interesting experiment to develop a new reputation for myself that didn't rely so much on levity. I'd have to try it out with a preliminary test subject, of course, and the new kid would be the perfect person to start with. Maybe I could also spin the dorky bloody-nose thing into something mysterious with someone who didn't know me.

If, of course, I could get the kid to look at me. I glanced from my own reflection to the other one in the mirror. Or at least I tried to. There was zero eye contact. Which was impressive in a pathologically shy kind of way because we were in a restroom with about four mirrors. Our faces were everywhere and yet we still weren't looking at each other.

"Oh, right, um—" The kid was completely flustered trying to put together a sentence and avoid the Hansel and Gretel–like trail of blood-not-bread I had left in my wake. Oops, me and my bloody philtrum were inciting fear rather than awe; scaring, rather than impressing, the kid. Better take it down a notch, lighten the moment with a joke or two, help make this new kid feel more at ease with me before both of us had stress-induced bloody noses and the room looked like a gory crime scene. I was forced back to being my typical quick-witted and entertaining self before ever really trying on cool as a new image.

"It didn't come from a fistfight or, you know, a spontaneous aortic rupture." I paused for the chuckle that didn't come. "This school has zero tolerance for violence. Not to mention unsupervised cardiac bleeds." Another pause for the laugh. Another moment of comedic death by silence.

"That's . . . good?"

Geez, my comic timing wasn't even appreciated by a kid who was, I should point out, carrying around a backpack with a cat poking out of it. My sense of humor is quickly becoming wasted around here. No one in this entire building gets my kind of funny anymore. I might have to transfer, try to find a middle school that's a better fit for someone with the gift of the wisecrack like me.

"What happened?" The kid was peering at my bloody tissue with the same revulsion one might reasonably direct toward a person just returned from a serial murder spree or breaking down game after a particularly successful hunting trip.

"Bloody nose. A real gusher this time. What can I say? It's an imperfect world and I have a deviated septum." And I bleed when I get worried about peer group interaction. But no one needs to know that except me and my counselor, Cary, who came up with the phrase "peer group interaction" in the first place. I grabbed a roll of toilet paper, dropped it to the floor, and used my foot to wipe up most of the blood. "Good enough. Now it's just a smear."

From the kid's gag reflex after a quick glance at— and then away from—the blood on the floor, I was worried we were going to be dealing with another kind of bodily fluid in a sec. Nope, deep breath, nausea under control, brave attempt to keep the conversation going. "You know a lot of words for blood residue."

"I get a lot of nosebleeds." That's like saying the *Titanic* took on a little water. My counselor says it's from social anxiety. Cary's probably right, but I don't want to deal with that just yet. Cary calls that avoidance; I call it pacing myself. "A person can do a lot of thinking with their head back and a wad of tissue packed in each nostril." Good position to avoid facing reality and any kind of personal interaction, by the way.

"You make good use of your time."

Wow. Look at me: meeting a secret optimist who's gradually warming to me. My day is definitely picking up. "Hardly anyone ever says that about me. Thanks."

I heard Ms. Mahoney in the hallway yelling at the few kids still in the building this long after dismissal to take shelter. I'm guessing she was shouting at students; but a she-devil like that could have just as easily been bossing around teachers and coaching staff. Or even directing the principal if she thought he wasn't toeing the line.

"Did a teacher with a clipboard shove you in here?" I asked, and the kid nodded, looking nervously at the door as if Ms. M. was going to burst in and start ordering us to scrub toilets or clean the grout. Which wasn't completely unlikely; I've seen her do worse in the name of running a tight ship.

"That woman's meaner than a junkyard dog. No wonder they always assign her to detention duty; she's hardwired to strike terror in the hearts of, well, everyone. The good news is that we're totally safe from the storm if we're anywhere near her: She'll intimidate any bad weather, like an infantry regiment on the front line of battle." That's not at all true, of course, but it's the kind of reassuring thing a person tells someone whose nerves seem to be stretched a little tight. I'd know all about something like that. The kid was in excellent, and empathetic, company.

"Oh . . . well, that's good, I mean, everyone should be . . . I dunno, useful in some way."

"I'm Jordan."

"Avery."

"What're you doing hanging around school so late?"

"It, uh, was, ah, my first day." I wondered if Avery thought we got graded by how many extra syllables we

could cram in a sentence or if there was another reason for the hesitation. Like maybe clinical introversion
or social maladjustment. I know those phrases because
Cary suggested they might apply to me in our first ses-
sion.

"Thought so. I'd have remembered the cat."

"You're not supposed to see him."

"Oooooookaaaaaay. An *invisible* stuffed cat. Gotcha."
Who am I to judge? But bingo on the call of maladjustment. Takes one to know one, I guess. "That still doesn't
explain what you're doing in school forty minutes after
the last bell rang."

"I hid backstage in the auditorium and fell asleep."

Interesting. "When?"

"As soon as I got here this morning. I slept all day."
No wonder the kid was a twitching wreck. "Is it still considered an official first day if I was sleeping under a costume rack instead of going to class?"

No, my new and trembling friend, you are toast.
Instead, I looked thoughtful, pretended to consider the

plight carefully, and then nodded. "You were on school property so, technically, you were present. No worries, you're good."

"Why are you still here?"

"I'm always here. If I were not here, there'd be no here here. The detention hall would cease to exist if I were not given detention several times a week. The faculty in this school doesn't get my humor. Apparently, I come off as difficult and challenging to authority."

"That's too bad. A good sense of humor is an important quality to have."

Ah. Socially awkward, but promising. Just like me. "You'd think. But wit like mine is wasted in the eighth grade. My counselor says it doesn't pay to be subversive in middle school."

Before my new potential BFF could respond or I could rip out my own tongue for admitting I see a counselor, the washroom door slammed open. Avery practically leapt into my arms but settled for scurrying behind me as a shield.

I turned away from the huddled mess that was Avery hiding behind me and saw who'd entered the restroom. Oh, right: Taylor. Good call, Avery. Everyone should duck and cover when Taylor enters the room.

"If you don't cut that out, I'll squash you like a bug." Taylor's not anyone's idea of charming. This was, in fact, one of Taylor's warmer utterances of the week.

Devon, the recipient of Taylor's warning, followed Taylor into the bathroom. Devon hasn't heard anything anyone's said for years, so, although a threat was delivered, a threat most certainly wasn't received. Devon was wearing earbuds and playing air guitar. Like always. I really mean it: ALWAYS. Even in class, albeit quietly and as discreetly as it is possible to rock out on an imaginary Fender Stratocaster. Or was it a Gibson? Hard to tell when, you know, it doesn't exist.

Normally, when I find myself in a small-group situation, I get very uncomfortable. But here, in this bathroom, with these people, I felt right at home, even though I'd just met Avery, Taylor is unpleasant, and

Devon doesn't communicate with people who can be seen. I was, far and away, not the only flaky one in the room, and that brought a level of social comfort I don't usually experience.

Taylor was still waiting for Devon to respond. Dream on, Taylor.

As if it would help clarify their communication process, such as it was, Taylor bellowed at Devon, "DID YOU HEAR ME?"

Devon not only hadn't heard anything anyone has said for years, but Devon had also lost the ability to read body language and facial cues. So the fist-into-palm-smacking and red angry face that Taylor was demonstrating as an example of seething rage fell on deaf, or earbud-stuffed, ears. Devon looked up from the guitar, smiled at Taylor, pumped both fists in the air like a rock star, and wandered into a stall to continue playing, one hoped, rather than to partake of the intended purposes of the facilities. Although we were *in* the bathroom, I sincerely hoped no one would have to *use* the bathroom.

Until the storm was over and the rest of us could leave, of course.

"I wish Devon was playing an actual guitar," Taylor snarled. "Then at least I could smash it in a million pieces."

And tell me the brand name if you happened to notice it among the splintered pieces of guitar. But that's not really the point, I reminded myself, and decided that a six-string connoisseur like Devon would go Fender all the way.

Mason had entered the room behind Taylor and Devon and been watching Taylor disapprovingly. "Some people have no appreciation for the musical arts. It's sad. Hey, Jordan." I nodded my hello and then gestured to Avery who was still crouched behind me. Mason leaned over, peeked behind my legs, and waved. "Hi, we haven't met—I'm Mason. I like the stuffed cat."

"You're not supposed to see it," I said helpfully.

"That's cool," Mason casually brushed off the not-really-there stuffed cat like it was the kind of thing someone was asked to ignore every day and, therefore, too trite to waste words mentioning. "I got you covered on the not-seeing-the-cat deal. Very metaphysical; I like it. Have you met Taylor and Devon yet?"

I looked over my shoulder at Avery and said, again very helpfully, "Taylor's hostile and Devon's mellow so they make a nice matched set. An ideally balanced sub-set of the collection of people to be stuck with in the bathroom during a storm."

Avery didn't know who to watch, the furious Taylor who was glaring at Devon or Devon who was playing so hard the strumming arm was windmilling. I noticed that Avery started anxiously twisting the cat's ears, which were poking out of the bag.

Clearly, an introduction to the Land o' Devon was in order for our new friend. The rest of us have gotten used to Devon's musical obsession and disdain for engaging on the plane of mutual reality, but, to the uninitiated, Devon might be a tiny bit crazy and, perhaps, a whole lot scary.

"Devon's the best musician in school," I said with a little pride even though I had nothing to do with Devon's talent. "The only problem is Dev's never so much as touched a real guitar. But look at that showmanship! A forward-thinking entrepreneur would send that act on the road, charge a modest admission at small clubs. Who knows? Maybe even work Dev up to an international major stadium tour gig, opening for world renowned rock gods."

And then *maybe* said agent/manager/promoter would notice the droll, and, I think, extremely marketable, humor that is mine and book me a job or series of jobs warming up the in-studio audience for one of the bazillion late-night talk shows. After Cary and I worked through my stage fright, that is. Maybe Devon's bizarre enough to land both of us at the top of the heap, entertainment career–wise. I'm not counting on it, but I'm not ruling it out, either. Devon might be my ticket to international fame and obscene fortune, or at least widespread social acceptance in this school. Again, if

Cary and I can work on getting me able to talk to people without resorting to acerbic commentary that masks my discomfort.

"Your faith in Devon has always been very touching, Jordy," Mason said with an approving smile.

"It's your fault Devon's still wandering around like this, Jordan; you encourage bad behavior to take the focus off of yourself." Leave it to Taylor to ruin the warm bonding moment we were all sharing. Taylor is exactly like the prank no one sees coming in the middle of the night on the way to the bathroom—unpleasant, abrasive, and shocking.

"Taylor, that was uncharacteristically aware of you," Mason said, and, bitter though I was about the point, I had to agree. "A little mean, but good eye: Jordan, no offense, *does* throw others under the bus to avoid the consequences of having a smart mouth and an all-around disrespectful attitude."

Before I could say, "Well, yeah, sure, who doesn't," or even bust Mason's chops for being hyperintellectual enough to make condescending comments like that in the first place, the door flew open again. My eardrums reverberated painfully from the noise. No wonder Devon likes to play guitar in the restroom—great sound quality and a nice echo.

"Can you believe we're stuck in the john because of a little rain? Coach canceled practice because of *drizzle* and a *light breeze.*" Regan would practice in a hurricane if necessary and doesn't take kindly to any changes in what has got to be the world's most carefully mapped out weekly schedule. Regan's the most active kid in this school. Between sports, student government, editing both the yearbook and the newspaper, participating in the plays and musicals, rehearsing for the orchestra and band concerts, serving on numerous school committees, volunteering in the community, and whatever else I'm sure I've forgotten, Regan has every spare moment of the day accounted for until high school graduation and that includes summer vacation and winter and spring breaks.

Regan noticed Devon flailing around on air guitar, studied the fingers on the frets and the rhythm, and then guessed, "Santana?" Mason and I nodded—good guess. Taylor snorted and turned away because that's Taylor's response to everything. Avery kept nervously twisting the cat's ears. Apparently neither Avery nor the stuffed cat wanted to weigh in on Devon's instrumental inspiration today.

"Better than pretending to be Hendrix, pretending to set the pretend ax on fire," Regan held up a flat palm in a *don't-go-there* gesture. "Now *that's* crazy. Speaking of crazy, what's with the kid petting the stuffed cat in the bag?"

"That's Avery," Mason said. "First day here. Seems a little more anxious than crazy."

"And we're not supposed to call attention to the cat. It's the exact opposite of Devon's guitar," I once again helpfully pointed out. Man! I have got to get a job being helpful; it comes so naturally to me, I may as well start getting paid for it.

"Which we're not supposed to *see* so much as *hear*," Mason commented on Devon's guitar, head tipped, eyes closed, face scrunched in a look of intense concentration, trying really hard, I guessed, to listen for the chords.

"There's a lot of existential reality in this school," I told Avery, and hoped I seemed French and intellectual and maybe a little brooding.

"I'm okay with that non-cat and the non-guitar," Regan said, looking back and forth between Avery and Taylor. "Maybe we can get a picture for the yearbook of Avery and Devon and the nonentities; as editor-in-chief this year, I'm freaking out about how to fill up all the pages. I'll take anything. Even pictures of invisible felines and imaginary stringed instruments."

"Everyone in this school except me is nuts," Taylor sneered.

"And yet you're the only one in this room failing," Mason broke the seal on that secret. "C'mon, Taylor, get your books out, let's finish that book report so we can be one step closer to being free of each other once and for all."

"Mason is tutoring Taylor," Regan explained to Avery.

"Taylor's resisting," I clarified, because I didn't think Regan's commentary gave Avery the full picture. "If Mason were a germ and Taylor were an open wound, Taylor would be studied by the worldwide medical community as the future hope of preventing the spread of infectious disease."

"Mason's only working with Taylor to get a recommendation from the principal to attend the mock congress in Boston this summer," Regan told the one person in this entire school who didn't already know about Mason's academic pursuits and extracurricular goals. The rest of us hate Mason for wrecking grade curves, for making all of us look like dopes with the constant extra credit assignments, for always taking all of the honors courses that are offered, and for having a study room in the library on permanent hold for whatever small-group project Mason has once again volunteered to head.

"They can't stand each other. Two people who loathe each other more do not exist in this world or any universe known to mankind or yet to be discovered. It's awesome entertainment for the rest of us that they have to work together. We've placed bets on how long it'll take one to smack the other with a thesaurus, and who'll take the first swing." I wondered what the current over-under was on Taylor drawing first blood.

"Our school policy is zero tolerance for bullying, so if I should personally witness such behavior, in my role as student body president, I'd have to report it. Was it *report it* or *step in*? Hmm, can't remember." Regan tried to look as anti-bullying and pro-getting-along as possible. Which just meant trying out a few different kinds of weird and eager smiles in the mirror combined with a furrowed brow for seriousness.

Mason looked up at the ceiling in disgust. "Taylor's failing English. Our mother tongue. My whole future depends on teaching someone the difference between *I-T-S* and *I-T*-apostrophe-*S*."

"I'm not failing," Taylor said. "I'm just not passing by as much as I should be. And you said 'it' was an imprecise and meaningless word that takes up space and should be avoided as much as possible. So what's the big difference if there's an apostrophe or not if I'm not supposed to use the word in the first place? Geez."

For a second I thought I was going to lose money when Mason grabbed a book. But the swing never came; instead of whacking the side of Taylor's head with a good solid backhand, Mason placed the book in Taylor's hand with a heavy sigh. "Focus."

Scene Two:

LOUDSPEAKER ANNOUNCEMENT: *"This is a weather update: The severe weather alert for the county immediately adjacent to ours is in effect until four thirty p.m. We are advised that strong winds are moving westward and that occasional rain or thundershowers are forecast with possible street flooding in low-lying areas. Total rainfall amounts are projected to vary between one to two inches."*

"Isn't that, like, a miniscule amount of precipitation that's hardly even noticeable?" I asked. "I swear, this school is the drama queen of the entire district—always making a big deal out of nothing. It's not like anyone just reported seeing animals walking two by two to get on a big boat; it's not *that* kind of storm."

"Better safe than sorry." Regan probably sat on the

student-faculty committee that came up with these dipsy-doodle rules in the first place. "I hope they let us out soon, though; I've got to get over to the senior center by dinnertime because I'm volunteering today. Speaking of dinner: I'm starving. Anyone got anything to eat?"

"You're going to eat in the bathroom? Next to a stall? Eww." But I had to admit: My stomach was rumbling too. I dug in my backpack and came up with some trail mix that I threw over to Regan.

"It's not like I was planning to suck water out of the toilet." Regan tossed a raisin in my mouth like I was a one of the seals at the zoo. Eating and throwing things pass time when you're bored. It's a scientific fact. Or at least universally accepted. Throwing things you can catch in your mouth and then eat adds to the fun.

Avery looked across the room and made a small squawk of alarm. "Devon is lying down on the floor. Why is Devon lying down on the floor like that?"

Regan, Mason, Taylor, and I glanced over at Devon and, in one voice, replied, "Acoustic set."

Avery looked blank. Well, sure, first time at this rodeo, who wouldn't be a little confused?

"Devon's resting while the lead vocalist takes the spotlight; it's only for one song. See!" I reassured Avery as Devon jumped up and started playing again.

"Oh. Okay," Avery said, looking neither comforted by nor comfortable with the fact that Devon is a generous band member who gives everyone onstage equal opportunity to shine.

In fact, Avery was starting to look more and more uncomfortable. Regan and I were gobbling trail mix and balancing peanuts on our noses when we weren't catching things in our mouths, Mason and Taylor were elbow-jabbing each other into slightly cracked or at least permanently bruised ribs while they huddled over a notebook and tried to hammer out a book report for a novel I'm pretty sure Taylor didn't read all the way through, and Devon was off riffing in the corner.

But Avery was restlessly shifting back and forth from one foot to the next and compulsively checking the time every forty-five seconds. And just when I'd thought we'd broken through the nerve thing and Avery was starting to feel comfortable with us. Bummer. Maybe it was just me who was starting to feel comfortable. Avery should try to be more like me. I'd have to set a good example for coping with the storm lockdown.

"So, that's it? We're stuck in the bathroom?" Avery sounded about ready to explode. I hoped that wasn't going to happen because a) I was starting to like Avery and b) I wasn't going to clean it up. Not enough toilet paper in the universe.

"Yup," I said, nodding, trying to role-model acceptance and patience with my relaxed attitude.

"For who-knows-how-long?" Avery wasn't following my lead and was, in fact, looking increasingly agitated.

"Looks that way," I said, again in a great-attitude-to-emulate way. I wished Cary could see how mature and easygoing I was, things I am never accused of outside of this lavatory.

"Pull up some floor, relax," Regan urged.

"And none of you are worried about the storm?" Avery asked, casting a panicked glance at the really small glass brick window above the sink.

"This school is known for overreacting about bad weather. Someone sees one teeny tiny bolt of lightning in the sky and the whole place is on lockdown. It's nothing." I remembered the Great Storm That Wasn't of seventh grade, when the entire student body had spent ages either sitting on the floor, lined up facing the wall, our arms over our heads, or crammed under our desks with faces tucked down, waiting for the building to collapse on top of us. Final tally: One branch was knocked off an ancient tree. Probably due to a fat squirrel rather than a dangerous gust of wind.

"Yeah, if it was really bad, they'd be telling us to hide under desks and cover our heads," Mason said, looking at me as if reading my mind. "Like that time last year, remember? This is sooooo not a big deal. The teachers haven't even checked on us."

"The weather cell will pass by and then someone will

get on the loudspeaker and announce we're free to go,"
Regan said in the most bored voice I've ever heard. "I
give the whole containment thing another twenty, thirty
minutes tops."

"I have to call my parents; they don't know where I
am. No one knows where I am." Avery was about a nanosecond away from totally flipping out. I sat up straight
and looked concerned and attentive—but still cool,
calm, and collected—hoping Avery would get the hint
and settle down.

"That's not entirely true; WE know where you are," I
said in my most consoling voice.

Regan, who is surprisingly emotionally tone deaf for
such a popular person, didn't get the invisible memo that
we were treating the skittish kid gently and, instead, poked
Avery in an already sore spot: "Besides, you're fourteen
years old—your folks aren't gonna freak out about where
you are at four o'clock in the afternoon on a school day."

"My parents freak out if I lock the bathroom door
when I take a shower."

As much as I wanted to be understanding and non-confrontational because of Avery's fragile state of mind and obvious panic at being trapped in the john during a storm, I couldn't keep from rolling my eyes when I heard that.

Avery saw my skepticism and tried to explain. "What if I slip on a bar of soap, hit my head, get knocked unconscious, land in the water that collects at the bottom of the tub after my forehead bumps the drain thing shut, and then drown because they can't get to me fast enough because they're having trouble trying to unlock the door with a Phillips head screwdriver?"

"And they think that's a likely scenario?" I wondered what kind of family Avery came from if that was the logical conclusion to their kid wanting a little me-time in the shower.

"My parents have heard of stranger things happening."

Sometimes Taylor's lack of a filter gets to the heart of the matter in a way diplomacy never can. Like this time: "Your parents are neurotic." Then Taylor turned to Mason and smirked. "Hah! Neurotic: vocab word."

"Now spell it." Mason is very hard to impress. I was on Taylor's side in this situation.

"You're a buzzkill," Taylor said. "I used it correctly in a sentence. And I keep telling you: I don't need to know how to spell."

"Yes, you do. We've gone over this before. Spellcheck on your computer is not the same thing as knowing how to spell." If a person could expire from sheer frustration, I think we would have had to figure out how to store Mason's body until we were released from the Non-Storm Watch-for-Nothing.

Avery, who wasn't nearly as worried about Mason's will to live as I was, started pacing, collar-tugging, hands-through-hair-running; your basic gestures indicating full-on panic mode. Avery would be a great charades partner; very readable clues and expressive movements.

Even Regan finally noticed Avery's agitation. "You okay?"

"Not really," Avery's eyes got huge. "Is it just me or does this room seem to be running out of, I don't know, oxygen?"

"Highly unlikely." I took a deep breath to demonstrate how oxygen-rich the room was. "Yep, oxygen levels seem fine to me. Look at my hands: My fingertips and nailbeds are nice and pink which means my O2 saturation is good."

"Are you getting claustrophobic? Do confined spaces make you uncomfortable?" Regan apparently never heard that people, especially edgy people under stress, are highly susceptible to the power of suggestion and that you should always offer positive ideas and never give them more grist for the crazy mill. Like offering up additional crises to factor in to the already tense and, let's face it, unstable, mix.

"Not as much as the lack of air. Can we open a window?" Avery eyed the window above the sink. I wondered if Avery was thinking about trying to chisel one of the glass bricks free to try to suck in some additional fresh air. I had a compass in my backpack that might help.

"During a storm?" Taylor snorted. "And people think *I'm* the dumb one."

"No one thinks you're dumb," I said. "We think you're disagreeable. Maybe even a little abusive."

Mason protested: "I think Taylor *might* be dumb. I think we can't entirely rule out that possibility."

Regan finally noticed that Avery was starting to actually pant in fear, and dug deep for a little human compassion: "Sit down and put your head between your knees, breathe deep and slow. We'll all just breathe together, calmly. No one's going to panic or run out of air." Regan was speaking slowly and carefully, like a hypnotist putting someone under, gesturing to the rest of us to start breathing together too. "It's allllllllllll gooooooooooood. Verrrrrry comforting and laaaaid baaaaaaack."

The room was silent. Mason, Taylor, Regan, and I were quietly breathing, synching our breaths, soothing Avery down together like some Zen crisis-response team. We were a nanosecond away from busting out some yoga poses and chanting.

Until Devon shattered the silence with an ear-piercing, blood-curdling, toe-curling, heart-stopping, mind-numbing shriek: "ROCK AND ROLL!"

I looked up and all I could see of Devon were finger-snapping and head-bobbing. Devon was twirling in a funky shuffle-slide across the floor, head back, eyes closed, complete abandon.

"Thanks, Dev, way to add to the tranquil atmosphere."

Devon couldn't hear me, but fist-pumped and danced in circles as if to agree.

Despite the fact that my heart hurt really bad because of the sudden stop/pause/restart that had just occurred because of Devon's unexpected bellow, I couldn't help but admire the unselfconscious joy of a musician in the midst of a heavy groove.

Although the moment was clearly over—our brief blip into the serene enlightenment of third-eye-opening meditation was a thing of the past—and we were back to being a bunch of tense middle schoolers hunched next to the toilets, it wasn't half bad to sit there watching Devon jam.

I've been to real concerts before—you know, professional musicians, actual instruments, audible music—that were a lot less fun that sitting on the bathroom tiles watching Devon air-guitar.

Devon was smart; all you ever hear is about how more traditional musicians and bands have legal hassles with their management or financial disagreements with their labels and distribution problems and struggles to get air time on the radio. But Devon's artistic freedom and creative integrity were still intact.

Apparently, there's a lot to be said for marching to the beat of one's own drum. Or guitar, as the case may be.

Scene Three:

"Hey, I know!" Regan bounced off the floor and looked as enthusiastic as only a natural-born leader can. Regan's probably been waiting for a chance like this for ages, ever since the webinar on how to rally the morale of the masses during a crisis. "Let's take our minds off being trapped in the bathroom. Taylor, put the book down and come over here. Wanna be like King Tut?"

Regan grabbed a roll of toilet paper from the shelf next to the sinks and started wrapping Taylor from head to foot and then tossed Avery another roll. "Here. Make a mummy cat. The ancient Egyptians used to bury their pets with them, so it's historically valid, plus you'll feel better with something to do."

Why we didn't think of wrapping up Taylor years ago,

I'll never guess. I had a brief image flash through my mind of using strips of newspapers dipped in paste instead of TP, turning Taylor into a ginormous piñata. Or at least paste over Taylor's mouth, just until the storm passed. Or until we graduated and went our separate ways.

We didn't have newspapers and paste, so Mason and I started tossing toilet paper at each other, like two-person juggling, keeping three rolls in the air at all times. Avery wrapped the cat in layers of toilet tissue and started to smile as it looked more and more like a tiny dead ancient Egyptian house pet. I could tell that the previously ragged breathing had started to regulate when Avery started humming happily.

"Thanks. I do feel a little better."

"Sure you do," Mason said. "Always good to keep your hands busy. Takes your mind off your worries."

"So does talking." I was dropping more rolls than I was catching or throwing so it was time to turn this boat around. I'm not very athletic or coordinated, but I am articulate and clever. "Let's play 'would you rather?'! Mason, would you rather have a job cleaning up after a kangaroo with loose bowels or live in a sweaty giant's work boots?"

"I would rather not play 'would you rather.' Regan, poke an airhole in the toilet paper so Taylor can breathe. I'm pretty sure someone like Taylor doesn't have any brain cells to spare."

"Okay, then, how about 'guess who it is by the smell of their armpits'?" I should work for a toy company; I am never at a loss for something to do, I am a veritable font of good ideas for amusement. Lucky for these guys I was there.

"No fair." Regan did a quick pit sniff. "I just ran laps before the weather got bad. I stink like fetid death."

"Good point." I sniffed and actually smelled Regan's point. Eww. "How about 'truth or dare'? Truth: What's the most embarrassing thing you've ever done?"

"Brought a stuffed cat to school on my first day."

"Well, since you mentioned it: What's the deal?" Mason stole a peek at the cat who was mummy-wrapped and still half-poking out of Avery's bag.

GARY PAULSEN

Avery started in on that multiple syllable thing so I knew, for some reason, the nerves were kicking in again. "Oh, uh, well, my, uh, my little brother must have, uh, hidden it in my bag this morning. Just snuck it right in there without me even noticing. Because I was worried about the new school."

"That was thoughtful. Has it helped?" Regan sounded like the answer was obvious: Hadn't helped a bit.

"If you consider sleeping through the whole day helping, then, yeah, huge assist."

"Again, since you brought it up, why'd you sleep all day?" I asked.

"I only meant to nap through science. They were dissecting fetal pigs." Avery looked miserable at the thought of baby pigs on the business end of a scalpel.

"Squeamish?" Regan, who is squeamish about nothing and could probably perform a self-appendectomy if it meant saving some time and not screwing up the schedule, asked.

"No. Vegan. I'm not down with animal rights

38

violation. I don't ingest, wear, or partake in the use of animals." Avery lifted a foot to demonstrate. "Even my shoes are made of canvas and hemp and contain no animal products, by-products, or derivatives."

"Why?" A life without cheeseburgers and belts; I couldn't imagine still wanting to live.

"Because well-planned vegan diets have been found to offer protection against many degenerative conditions, including heart disease."

"And that's a legitimate concern for a kid in middle school?"

"My parents have heard of weirder things happening."

Good thing I hadn't whipped out a leg of lamb or a rack of pork ribs to gnaw on when Regan asked if I had food. That might have sent Avery clear around the bend. I tried to hide my leather sneakers and wondered what other animal parts I might inadvertently be wearing. Pretty sure jeans aren't made of anything that once had a face. If asked, I'd lie and say my shoes were made old string and recycled tennis balls or something.

Taylor proved that a mask of toilet paper was not nearly enough to enforce silence, and mumbled, "Mmmumph gurrrrble dunderschmickzen."

"Yeah, what Taylor said: How did 'science class' become 'all day long'?" Taylor and Mason have been spending wuh-hay too much time together if Mason could translate what Taylor had just garbled.

"Once you've gone to sleep at school and missed a class or two—or five—it's kind of hard to find the correct reentry point," Avery said. "Every time I woke up, I worried about calling attention to myself by showing up late to class. So I just rolled over and went back to sleep."

"Timing *is* everything," I said. "A good entrance is essential when you're attempting to make a strong first impression. I'm feelin' you." I never believe my entrance and exit lines are strong enough. I frequently wish life had do-overs. Because then I could kill with the perfect one-liner—I never think of the perfect response until way after the moment has passed.

"Devon's lying down on the floor again. Another acoustic set?" Avery wasn't panicked so much as curious this time. Amazing how fast someone adjusts to Devon's concerts.

"Intermission." Regan, Mason, and I got up and stretched.

"Sure, I should have guessed." Avery watched as Devon leapt up and started playing again and said, in an announcer-like voice: "Annnnnnnnnnnnnd welcome to the second half of the show."

The loudspeaker squawked again. Not so much because anyone in a position of authority was terribly concerned with our comfort level or because we needed to know what was going on, but because it gave the school limited culpability in case of a lawsuit. In case anyone got blown to another state or ruined their shoes in a mud puddle, it was not the school's fault.

"Occasional gusts of wind are moving west at nearly three miles per hour. They pose no immediate threat to this area. In the interest of the safety of the population of this school,

however, please remain where you are. Until we are assured that all danger has passed, do not emerge from your safe location in an interior room, away from windows and flying objects."

In one of those perfect moments that you dream of experiencing and never forget (everyone, except, of course, for Taylor, who was still wrapped in toilet paper, blinded and immobile) I immediately and wordlessly picked up the nearest roll of toilet paper and hurled it at Taylor. This should be a carnival game; people, at least in this school, would pay big bucks to chuck stuff, even soft stuff, at a helpless Taylor.

"I'm sure they meant *dangerous* flying objects." I led the high-fives all around.

Taylor ripped the toilet paper away and took a deep breath, glaring at each of us in turn. "What stinks in here?"

"Probably me." Regan grinned. "I repeat: Just came off the track after running laps."

"It might be that we're in a restroom and you don't actually smell anything so much as the environment is highly suggestive to the existence of a malodorous scent." Mason's not the only one who can trot out big words to confuse people. I have a dictionary, too, you know, and can use fancy vocabulary to confound people when it amuses me.

Taylor looked gratifyingly confused and confounded. "Hunh?"

"Jordy means you're imagining things, Taylor." Mason shot a tiny glare at me for stealing the big-word thunder although I was the only one who noticed. "I don't smell anything." Then Mason took a deep sniff for emphasis and course-corrected. "Oh, wait, scratch that: I *do* smell something funky."

We all checked out the air quality and then looked at each other suspiciously and edged away from the stalls. Taylor peered in the trash can, but discovered no source of stink there.

"It's puke," I suggested.

"Nah, it's toe jam," Taylor said.

"Nope." Regan went the stinky cheese route, because

what middle schooler doesn't bring reeking, imported, runny dairy product sandwiches to lunch instead of a PB&J? "Limburger cheese."

"You're all wrong," Mason said, wincing. "It's goat pee and used cat litter and fresh skunk and rotten chicken."

Avery looked around, did a double-take, and took a tentative whiff of the mummy cat, before looking embarrassed and shoving the cat back in the duffel bag. "Uh, actually it's the stuffed cat."

"Your stuffed cat?" Taylor asked.

"No, Taylor, the stuffed cat that the builders put in the air vents for good luck and to drive away bad spirits. How many stuffed cats do you imagine we're dealing with here? Today? In this restroom?" Now it was Mason's turn to be the high-maintenance person in need of calming down. Mason's patience, at least with Taylor, was nearing an end.

"Is that a trick question?" Taylor looked worried and then thoughtful. "Like that Venn diagram thingie you tried to show me? Are there somehow three cats in circles and there's an overlap of the stinky and the nonstinky and the possibly stinky cats I'm supposed to figure out?"

"One cat, Tay." I held up my index finger as a visual aid.

"I knew it! I was right! I'm not always wrong, no matter what Mason says." Taylor looked triumphant about having solved the cat word problem.

"Why does your cat stink like death, Avery?" Regan asked. Probably wondering where to get one so as not to be the stinkiest thing in every room. I'm not sure Regan schedules enough showers or deodorant applications in the weekly agenda. It's not something I'd say out loud, because Regan is a great person, but it's something I've been thinking for quite some time now.

Avery gave up the extra syllables thing and went for hyper-speed as the nerve burn-off delivery system this time. "It's not my cat; it's my brother's cat, he's only four. Four year olds have stuffed cats. It's perfectly normal. For a four year old. But I have no idea why it reeks like this. It doesn't normally smell like vomit."

"Apparently, confined spaces combined with the warmth of your head resting on the bag all day adversely altered the chemical compound of whatever the stuffed cat was originally stuffed with, turning it into a rancid stink bomb," I said, glad I'd paid attention in science class and could whip out theories and theorems and hypotheses when needed, like in The Case of the Mysteriously Putrid-Scented Stuffed Cat. "There are some extra credit science points in there somewhere if you figure out the hows and the whys of the mystery stench. I'm just saying—you might need some bonus projects to submit, seeing as how you cut class today."

Avery nodded, looking happy, and took out a notebook, jotting down, no doubt, my brilliant suggestion. Mason leaned over and scribbled down what looked, from my vantage point, like a phone number; Mason's either a glutton for punishment or can't, apparently, let anyone do their homework unassisted. Mason handed the notebook to Taylor who, surprisingly enough, wrote a number down too. Taylor handed the pen to Regan who, I noticed, wrote down two numbers—someone had to bring Devon into the mix, it wasn't time for another set break yet. I wrote my number down when the book made its way to my hands and made sure I had everyone's number in my phone. I looked up and saw I wasn't the only one punching digits in my phone's contact list.

Funny—Mason, Taylor, Regan, Devon, and I have gone to school together forever and this was the first time we all made sure we had each other's numbers.

I studied Avery, who was starting to look a lot less like an overwrought curiosity with a soft toy and a lot more like the reason this little group of mismatched misfits was coalescing into Team Riding Out the Storm Together in the Bathroom.

Maybe the cat's stench was some sort of magic potion that brought unexpected people together.

I'm sure Avery's folks would say weirder things have happened.

Scene Four:

One of the best parts about hanging around Devon is that, when there's a lull in the conversation, no one's necessarily bored or even uncomfortable; we just shift our attention to observing Devon's gig. Being near Devon means never having to experience an awkward silence or struggle to come up with something to say. When we run out of conversation topics, we just settle back and watch the show. Everyone should have a Devon in their lives; we're just lucky we have the original.

Devon didn't let us down; it was solo time.

Devon switched from air guitar to a combination of air drums and air piano, twisting back and forth slamming the drum heads and pounding the keyboards. Devon held up both hands, ring and middle fingers tucked under the thumbs, index and small fingers up in the rock-and-roll sign, twirling in circles and head-banging to a beat no one else could hear.

Except we could all feel it. We were rocking back and forth to the rhythm. Even Taylor's head started nodding in time. Eventually, Devon moved away from the keyboard and drum kit and started playing the guitar again. Solo over, Devon wandered back to the corner of the bathroom in what was, clearly, the upstage area where, at least in Devon's universe, the roadies probably stood by with bottles of artesian spring water and a new box of guitar picks, maybe a towel to wipe the sweat off Devon's face.

"Don't take this the wrong way, but does anyone ever wonder if there's something not quite right with Devon?" I felt a lot like Taylor asking that so I made sure to have a friendly voice. I didn't want anyone to think I was being judgmental. I was just curious. It sounds weird, but I'd never taken the time to ask anyone's opinion about the Devon situation before. You don't ask what people think about gravity; it's just there, doing its thing, everyone is aware, but no one really discusses it. Just the way, when you come to think about it, we blindly accept and never question the weird alchemy that makes up Devon.

"You mean because of the way Dev doesn't seem to live in the same world as the rest of us?" Regan was studying Devon as if this was the first time we'd all laid eyes on our silent musician friend.

I nodded. "I love Dev—what's not to love about Dev, right?—and it's not like Devon hasn't been like this since kindergarten and we've all gotten used to things but, you know, looking at the situation with fresh eyes, a person starts to wonder."

"What I wonder is why Devon's even at school this late anyway," Mason said, studying Devon, too. "Taylor and I were in the library, researching; Regan was at practice and Jordy was in detention because that's where Regan and Jordan always are; and Avery was asleep—but does anyone know why Devon was still roaming the halls playing guitar so long after school was dismissed?"

"Devon missed the bus. And I don't mean just today." Taylor turned, looked at Mason, and smirked. "It's a metaphor."

"Spell it," Mason dared. "And if you use an *F*, I'll throw my shoe at you." But even Mason seemed more preoccupied with watching Devon than taunting Taylor. With that in mind, we might need to send Devon to the United Nations to broker some peace between other warring factions.

"It doesn't take a third-year psych student to figure out Dev's the teeniest, tiniest bit touched in the head, as my great-aunt Blanche would say," Regan said gently. We all nodded and kept watching Devon wander around strumming.

"We haven't actually spoken—Devon *can* hold a conversation, right?" Avery asked and we shrugged in reply; truth be told it had been a while since any of us had spoken to or heard from Devon. The best we could do at this point was guess. "But I get the feeling Devon's a good person. I like people who are different."

"Then you are in the right middle school restroom with the right five people." I looked around. "Because, not to brag or anything, but you could not have set out to gather together a group of people who are more unhinged than us."

I didn't think I was exaggerating; I couldn't think of a more unlikely group to find themselves together in a more unexpected set of circumstances unless Pebbles Flintstone, Napoleon, Elvis Presley, a Sherpa from Mount Everest, Marie Curie, and the shark from *Jaws* decided to stage a coup on the constitutional monarchy of the principality of Liechtenstein and form a new ruling government.

"Speak for yourself." Regan looked and sounded offended that I'd pointed out the obvious by stating we were an odd bunch. "I am the very definition of the clean-cut, all-American scholar-athlete young citizen role model. The fact that I am wickedly good-looking and heart-meltingly charming is a happy bonus."

"Regan took more than one person's share while standing in the self-confidence line," Mason explained to Avery while Regan nodded, trying to look humble. Mason decided to borrow a little of Regan's self-confidence and make a bold statement of self as well. "My only problem is that I might be too smart to fit in with my peers."

"Mason took more than one person's share while standing in the ego line," Taylor explained to Avery before turning to Mason. "And you spell *that C-O-N-C—E I*-before-*E*-except-after-*C T-E-D*."

I have to hand it to Mason, instead of getting offended, Mason applauded Taylor's insult. It was a pretty good one.

"The only problem I have," Taylor continued, "is a low tolerance for goofballs. Which, if you ask me, is pretty much everyone in this school."

"None of you are anything like the kids from my last school," Avery told us.

"What was that like?" I asked. I'd been wondering

what kind of school spit out such a jittery, sensitive mass of worry.

"It wasn't a school so much as a—now don't overreact to the word—but *commune.*"

In my wildest dreams, I hadn't seen *that* coming. "You're going to have to do some explaining."

"*Commune* might be the wrong word." Avery paused, considering. "A bunch of parents and their kids lived together as one big family, raising a garden for food and sharing all the responsibilities."

"*Commune* is the exact right word." I said, nodding. No wonder Avery had been weirded out about meeting new people; that was a whole lot of bizarre history to have to share with new people.

"We only lived there for a few months. Just to see what it was like. My folks like to try new things." Avery got my vote for biggest understatement of the day. I made a mental note to meet these parents someday and observe them up close. Because maybe the next new thing they'd want to try was counterfeiting hundred dollar bills or opening a gourmet chocolate shop out of their spare bedroom. A person would want to be around for stuff like that.

"Have you tried out any other alternative lifestyles we should know about? Other than that vegan thing you talked about before?" I'm sure Mason only wanted to know in case there was an extra-credit character study that could be turned in to English class: Interesting People I Met Near Toilets. Mason's always looking for ways to plump up the old GPA. Even if that meant exploiting the private lives of new friends by examining their origins and plumbing their family's beliefs.

"Like living in a tree house, maybe doing without electricity or prime numbers?" Taylor looked more interested in getting to the bottom of Avery's family life than I've ever seen Taylor get about anything.

"Taylor, I'm impressed. I don't believe you can actually *name* a prime number, but big props for knowing the phrase. We'll circle back to that concept later." Mason and Taylor high-fived.

"I could totally live off the land if I had to live in a commune," Regan said happily. "Hunting, fishing, building shelter."

"You could not." I popped the balloon of that dream real quick. "You were worried about starving to death during a storm emergency."

"That's because I was surprised and didn't have time to get all my gear together. Under normal circumstances, I'm known for my preparedness. Gotta be on top of things when you're in as many activities as I am."

"I can't believe we haven't voted you CEO of the school yet." I was half-joking, but Regan took me totally seriously.

"Me too! CEO, COO, CFO, and whatever other C-Os there are. I *am* the personification of school spirit in this building." Regan looked ready to do some more serious self-back-patting so I nipped that self-congratulatory excess in the bud.

"That's the kind of thing you generally let other people say; announcing it just makes you come off even more obnoxious than you already are."

"I know. But I don't let things like that get me down. I'm awesome that way." Regan paused to look in the mirror and gloat. "I am the most perfectly well-adjusted person you'll ever meet. Probably because I'm in a ton of activities and have more friends than anyone else."

"You say that like they're good things," I said, wishing I could beg, borrow, or steal a little of Regan's sense of assuredness.

"I say that like it's the secret to life. Which, by the way, it is."

Mason had been dying to say something and jumped in. "I think you're wrong, Regan, the secret to life is good grades and enrichment classes and advanced placement and extra credit. For a person like me. But, Jordan, if I were you, I'd listen to what Regan has to say."

Mason say what? When did this conversation take a hard right onto Talking About Jordan Boulevard? Maybe no one noticed and we'll keep talking about Avery and Regan, maybe throw in a little Mason and Taylor, swing back around to more discussion about

What Makes Devon Tick, or Strum. Totally abandon the Time to Study Jordan theme.

I looked at the floor and concentrated really hard: *Change the subject; veer off in a different branch of the conversation; no one's talking about Jordan. Jordan is of no interest, topic-wise.*

I swear I felt the entire vibe of the room shift because of the power of my mind. I sat back, sighing, and waited for my chance to jump in with an opinion about someone else at the soonest opportunity.

Scene Five:

No such luck.

Regan's got a one-track mind and the rails were headed directly toward me. Regan missed the whole energy shift of the room. My bad, I hadn't been facing Regan when I attempted to mind-control the population.

"Thanks, Mason." Regan dismissed Mason's contribution to the conversation. "We'll get back to you in a second. But first, semirhetorical question: Anyone notice that Jordan gets nosebleeds a lot?"

Oh snap. We're going there. No one has any idea how hard I've tried to avoid my bloody noses as a topic of conversation. Except maybe Cary, who gets paid to talk to me about them. And probably notices when I avoid the subject every week. "Yeah? So what?"

"I read that bloody noses can be a side effect of nerves," Regan said, staring at me as if I were an escaped mental patient about to get real interested in sharp objects.

It's not nerves, I told Regan—silently, in my mind. *It's excessive amounts of stress that are not addressed which lead to physical manifestations. Nosebleeds are considered one of these physical manifestations.* Out loud, I said, "I'm the least nervous person you'll ever meet, Regan. I'm an extrovert, in case you hadn't noticed. Class clown. Most likely to make people pee from laughing at my jokes."

Regan looked at me with the same expression my counselor has when I try to dodge the topic at hand by being flippant. And countered my statement, just like Cary does.

"You refused to try out for the school play when I asked you to keep me company at auditions."

"I found the play selection derivative and trite." I sounded calm, but I was starting to sweat buckets.

"You had a completely bogus excuse for why you couldn't be my partner on the debate team."

"What's bogus about the fact that it was a Thursday of a full moon week and my horoscope warned me to avoid oral conflict?" It's like no one in this school is guided by the wisdom of planetary alignment except me. Geez.

"You said you didn't have time to devote to being in the big buddy program with me at the elementary school." Regan is relentless. Why wasn't anyone else stepping in? I glanced around, but they were looking back and forth between us, watching the conversational tennis match, too interested in Regan's point and my counterpoint to break up the action by interrupting. Forty-love, advantage Regan. I gave it one last shot, though.

"That would have entailed afternoon meetings and, as you know, I've got a standing date with the detention hall." And with Cary for the alleged social anxiety thing my counselor thinks I have. I'm not socially anxious, I'm just wildly uncomfortable talking to more than one person at a time. Unless, it seems, it's in the second floor restroom of RJ Glavine Middle School. I was holding my own. Until, of course, Regan started in on me.

"You've never tried out for a single team even though I always invite you to go out for basketball, tennis, track, soccer, lacrosse, and golf when I'm being evaluated for the teams." Regan, clearly, doesn't mind being scrutinized by people while performing physical activity. That made one of us.

"What's your point?" I finally asked.

"My point is that I think you might be insecure."

Man! I hate being psychoanalyzed by a peer. Especially when they're right. "I'm just not into calling attention to myself. Unlike Devon." I shot a glance in Devon's direction.

By that point, Devon was leading a clap-along, arms overhead, clapping to a steady beat, as if rousing the crowd to get to their feet and join in for the best part of the song everyone's been waiting for the entire concert.

"Devon commits to the moment." Regan's face was positively glowing with admiration for Devon. It really ticked me off.

"Yeah, too bad Devon doesn't commit to reality." Even I winced at what a nasty thing that was for me to say and did a wordless gesture of apology, slapping my forehead and shaking my head in disgust. Everyone nodded, silently excusing me because they knew the heat of the moment had caused me to say something I didn't really mean.

"If I were to bet," Regan suddenly launched into a spot-on impression of Cary, "I'd say that you secretly wish you were more like Devon. Go on, and look me in the eye and tell me you don't dream of becoming a stand-up comedian. I'd put money on the fact that you practice one-liners in the bathroom mirror and take notes so you'll have funny things to say in conversations, don't you?"

Well, duh, didn't seem like the right thing to say, so I didn't say anything.

Avery piped up. "I think Regan makes a good point about you and Devon: One of you is living the dream; the other one has detention all the time and a lot of bloody noses."

We turned to study Devon who was rocking the neck of the guitar up and down, arching back as if in a backbend and then leaning forward in a crouch and prowling across the stage, bent over, knees bent, totally blissed out.

Avery had a point. A good one. And if this is what it was like to talk to a bunch of people at one time, I could deal with it, maybe it was growing on me. After all, my nose hadn't started oozing again the whole time we'd been together. And, although I'd been snarky, I hadn't offended anyone. Like I usually do. Which was a nice change of pace.

"Okay, you got me." I threw my hands up in defeat. "Clearly, we should all be more like Devon and Regan."

Regan reached in a file folder that appeared, seemingly out of thin air, and handed me a registration form for a talent show the drama club was putting on. Regan had already filled it out for me, all I had to do was add my signature. "Here." Regan grinned. "You can get over your fear of speaking doing a set at the fundraiser next week. You'll tell jokes for a good cause and overcome your performance anxiety by playing to a crowd bigger than one."

I signed my name before I could think about it and handed the form back. "So, I'm going to join at least one of Regan's extracurricular activities. Good thing it's the one that plays to my skill set: I'll be able to wander around telling random jokes, maybe even doing a few improv skits." I wheeled around as if facing a live audience and pointed. "You! Come up here on the stage next to me. An escaped convict, the grease trap of an Atlantic City casino's kitchen stovetop, and a misunderstanding about a blind date. Now improvise a scene with me using those ideas and . . . GO!"

"I actually think that sounds kind of amazing. I'll sign up and get involved if you will—probably easier if we have each other's backs. I'll be less likely to doze through another school day if I know someone's got my back around here."

We all turned to study Avery. Who, by the mere fact

of speaking and capturing our attention, had inadvertently, but undeniably, jumped onto the hot seat. Baton passed. It was now Avery's turn to face the merciless scrutiny of peer-group Q&A in the impromptu interrogation room that had, until recently, been the second-floor restroom of RJ Glavine Middle School.

Scene Six:

"You don't have a little brother, do you?" I asked Avery.

"No." Avery petted the cat poking out of the bag. And then smiled at it. Looked up from the cat and smiled at me. Relieved it was all coming out.

"The stuffed cat belongs to you, doesn't it?"

"Yeah. But not the puke smell. I don't know where *that* came from."

"Backstage," Regan explained. "You do not even want to know what happened after the musical last month. Thought we'd cleaned everything up. Guess not." *Actors are so careless,* I thought. *I'd never be that kind of sloppy performer.*

"Now that we all know the stuffed cat belongs to you, are you going to leave him at home?" I asked.

"Probably just get a bigger bag."

"That's what I figured." It's what I would have done.

"I love when stuff works out so I look like the really cool person with all the answers." Regan paused to reflect. "It happens a lot, but it never gets old."

"That's very chummy for you three and, no doubt, in the best interests of the entire school," Mason said, sounding impatient and totally out of the loop in terms of the magical bonding moments that had just occurred. "But Taylor and I have a book report to finish. Taylor, you have one last paragraph to write and then you're done. Then, today, when your mother asks you what you did today, you can say, 'Spared Mason from dying of frustration and boredom by finishing my homework assignment.' She'll be so proud."

"What about you, Mase?" Regan asked. "What are you going to tell your mom about what you and your friends did today?"

"She would never ask that. Because she knows that I don't have friends. I have well-connected contacts. And influential references. And helpful associates. And challenging academic colleagues."

"Nah. That's not all. You have friends." Was that a smile or bared teeth? With the old Taylor, it would have been a sign of aggression. But now, with the new and improved Taylor, I was going to go with the belief that it might actually be a smile. A real one. Mason was harder to convince.

"Right. You want me to believe that you actually stopped to think about whether or not I have a big enough social circle?" Mason's facial expression was somewhere between suspicious and doubtful.

Taylor carefully recited a list of numbers: "Two, three, five, seven, eleven, thirteen, seventeen, nineteen, and twenty-three."

I scratched my head and Regan looked stumped. Avery, however, was tickled to death by the newest turn of events. "Cool! First Devon tunes out and has a little concert going on in the corner. Then Jordan turns into a human punch-line generator. Now Taylor's become a number-spewing savant. You cannot tell me there isn't something really unique in the air at this school. Even my parents would not believe weirder things could happen."

I studied Mason's face. I saw confusion and a smile and wasn't sure what the overriding reaction to Taylor's number list was until I heard the admiration in Mason's voice. "No. That's not it; those are prime numbers. Taylor just listed *prime numbers*." Mason turned to Taylor and grinned. "You *have* been paying attention when we work together."

Taylor fake-scowled. "Not only is it hard to tune someone like you out, but—" Then Taylor took a deep breath and, in a very serious voice, said, "Concomitant with your mistaken belief that I'm not nearly as bright as you are, is the insulting way you have ignored the fact that I am ideal friend material."

Just when I thought the most interesting part of the day had already happened, a few times over, Taylor goes ahead and throws a new curve into the game. I held my breath, waiting to see what happened next.

"What did Taylor just say?" Avery poked me.

"*Is* that still Taylor?" Regan poked me from the other side.

"Shhhhh." I waved them off. "I want to hear Taylor explain why it was a good idea to play dumb just to cozy up to Mason." Because it sure wasn't anything I was going to figure out on my own.

"You pretended to be stupid so I'd tutor you?" Mason asked.

"Don't flatter yourself." Taylor's cheeks turned red. "I was struggling—a bit—to catch up after I had mono last term and I needed some help. For a while. A *little* while. But then I kind of liked hanging out with you; you're not so bad for an antisocial intellectual snob who doesn't have time for amigos."

"You have a weird way about you."

I wanted to retrieve the understatement of the year award I'd previously given to Avery and hand it to Mason for that line.

"Anyone can make a friend the old-fashioned way,

'hey, we have a lot in common and get along, wanna hang out and watch TV?' Boring. My way showed . . ." Taylor and Mason, vocab buddies and now, apparently, real life friends, too, finished the sentence together, "Panache."

The loudspeaker bleated: *"Attention! The storm warnings have been lifted for this entire area. The weather is clear and it is now safe to leave your secure area. Thank you for your cooperation."*

Oh.

Bummer.

The non-storm that never showed up and posed absolutely zero danger to anyone's safety had drawn to an anticlimatic end. And we were free to leave the second-floor restroom of RJ Glavine Middle School and go our separate ways.

Truth be told, I was a little disappointed it was over. I could tell that everyone else was too. You'd have thought we'd have made a break for the door the instant we were released, but we just stood there, looking at each other. No one knew what to do. Or say.

Which is when Devon stepped forward.

Dev came all the way downstage of whatever venue the band had been rocking, facing the audience that, I hoped, was going out of their minds screaming for the show, slipped the air guitar strap off, held it high in the air, and took a huge bow. "Thank you. Thank you very much. We hope you enjoyed our music. The band and I had a blast. You're a great audience. Rock on! We love you. See you next time. Drive home safely! Good night!"

Then Devon backed up, still facing whatever audience was waiting around for the encore, and grabbed the hands of the two closest people. They happened to be Avery and Taylor who immediately grabbed Mason and me in a tight grip so all five of us stood hand in hand. Devon pulled us all forward, closer to the edge of the stage, and led us in a group bow.

As we raised back up, all of us giggling and shoving each other, we shouted, one last time in the great sound-carrying room, "ROCK AND ROLL!"

Note from the author/ playwright:

Thinking, first thoughts, the beauty of ideas, thought-grow . . .

Sometimes, almost always, it comes when you are alone.

Alone.

Often just before sleep or just after you awaken, when the new day comes but before the business of life can rumble it up or when at night your body is tired and your mind is ready to rest, but not quite.

Not quite.

Then.

Just then it is there.

An idea.

They are so strange, ideas. A mental image, a thought, a wisp of a millionth of a volt of electric energy through brain cells to make a sound, a color or even just the tiniest memory of a color or sound or smell or taste or feeling.

Still, it is born. It is there, a kind of tool, and what comes of it is up to you, how you use the tool to make . . . to make whatever it is you want to make of it.

In a cave in France there are paintings that are twenty, thirty thousand years old. They are paintings of horses, bison, bears, and in one staggeringly powerful place, a man or a woman held a hand up to the cave wall and dabbed pigment around it to make an exact outline of the hand.

Signing the work with pride, with knowledge, with the idea that somehow, some day some other person will come into the cave and see this work, this idea, and will know that he or she of the hand is the one who made it, who found it and made it.

An idea.

A thought-idea for all of time, signed and ready to see.

And the effect that it has had is staggering. The paintings are admittedly beautiful but they have also led to almost countless other paintings, sculpture, whole movements of new cultures and thought on how those people lived, how they thought and felt and worshipped and loved and feared and knew, *knew* their world.

Twenty, thirty thousand years ago, twenty or thirty centuries in the past, so old that it was before there was even the concept of time. Right then a person had an idea, he or she formed it and decided to make it a painting on a cave wall.

But perhaps, just perhaps, it was more as well. Maybe it became a dance, where somebody put skins on their back and danced around the fire to tell what the hunt was like; or a song, a sung tale of the beauty of the large animals that were part of their lives, their dreams.

Their dreams.

Or maybe, just maybe it was a play. . . .

The Play:

SIX KIDS AND A STUFFED CAT

6 characters, male or female

STORY OF THE PLAY

Six middle-school kids find themselves together in a restroom, seeking refuge from an impending storm. Conversation is shared, secrets are revealed, friendships are formed, and plans are made, set to the imaginary soundtrack of classic rock-and-roll guitar hero music.

SIX KIDS AND A STUFFED CAT

A One-Act Play

by

Gary Paulsen

Produced by ....

Directed by ....

Staged by ....

With a company of six (and a half)

JORDAN ....

AVERY ....

TAYLOR ....

DEVON ....

MASON ....

REGAN ....

Adult voice on loudspeaker ....

List of props:

A couple pieces of facial tissue

One stuffed cat

A duffel bag or backpack per character

Earbuds

A few books and a couple of notebooks

A baggie of small snacks (raisins, trail mix, etc.)

A number of toilet paper rolls

And, of course,

Air guitar, air drums, and air keyboards

(guitar pick and drum sticks optional)

Setting:

Middle school restroom

RUNNING TIME: 17 minutes

SIX KIDS AND A STUFFED CAT

ACT ONE

Scene: JORDAN, about 14, leaning against the wall of a middle school restroom, dabbing nose with tissue.

    Time: After school.

SOUND CUE #1: LOUDSPEAKER ANNOUNCEMENT: Attention! A severe weather alert is likely to be issued for the surrounding areas. In the interest of erring on the side of caution and adhering to the guidelines of our prudent insurance liability policy, we strongly recommend that any faculty, staff, and students remaining in the school building immediately seek shelter in the nearest interior room. I repeat: Due to the slight possibility of potentially sudden onset heavy rain, please move immediately to a safe location, away from windows, and remain there until the all-clear sounds. Thank you.

(AVERY, same age, enters the lavatory from the hall, sees the first character, draws back, nervously trying to zip closed the duffel bag; a stuffed cat pokes out of the open flap. The indistinct sound of adult voices comes from offstage, teachers ushering errant students in various rooms along the hall for safety.)

JORDAN
(still dabbing at nose with tissue, to AVERY, who is hesitating by the door): Don't step in the blood.

AVERY
What?

JORDAN
You were about to walk right though the *(pauses for emphasis)* splatter. It's not nearly enough to be a *(pauses*

for emphasis) puddle, but it's more than a *(pauses for emphasis)* sprinkle.

AVERY

(wrinkling nose and shying away): Oh, right, um—

JORDAN

It didn't come from a fistfight or, you know, sponta-neous aortic rupture. *(pauses for laugh that doesn't come)* This school has zero tolerance for violence. Not to men-tion unsupervised cardiac bleeds.

AVERY

That's . . . good? *(peers at the floor, cringes, and then looks back at JORDAN)* What happened?

JORDAN

(still dabbing at nose): Bloody nose. A real gusher this time. *(shrugs)* What can I say? It's an imperfect world and I have a deviated septum. *(Takes roll of toilet paper*

and wipes the floor) Good enough. Now it's just a *(pauses for emphasis)* smear.

AVERY

You know a lot of words for *(pauses for emphasis)* blood residue.

JORDAN

I get a lot of nosebleeds. A person can do a lot of thinking with their head back and a wad of tissue crammed up each nostril.

AVERY

You make good use of your time.

JORDAN

Hardly anyone ever says that about me. Thanks. *(They nod at each other, you're welcome)* Did a teacher with a clipboard shove you in here? *(AVERY nods and looks anxiously at the door as if worried she'll enter)* That woman's meaner than a junkyard dog. No wonder they always assign her to detention duty; she's hardwired to strike terror in the hearts of, well, everyone. The good news is that we're totally safe from the storm if we're anywhere near her: She'll frighten any bad weather away, like an infantry regiment on the front line of battle.

AVERY

Oh . . . well, that's good, I mean, everyone should be . . . I dunno, useful in some way.

JORDAN

I'm Jordan.

AVERY

Avery.

JORDAN

What're you doing hanging around school so late?

AVERY

It, uh, was, ah, my first day.

JORDAN

Thought so. I'd have remembered the cat.

AVERY

(tucking the stuffed cat deeper in the backpack): You're not supposed to see him.

JORDAN

Oooooookaaaaaay. An *invisible* stuffed cat. Gotcha. *(They study each other for a long beat)* That still doesn't explain what you're doing in school forty minutes after the last bell rang.

AVERY

I hid backstage in the auditorium and fell asleep.

JORDAN

When?

AVERY

(worried): As soon as I got here this morning. I slept all day. Is it still considered an official first day if I was sleeping under a costume rack instead of going to class?

JORDAN

(pauses, considers, nods): You were on school property so, technically, you were present. No worries, you're good.

AVERY

(sighs, sags in relief): Why are you still here?

JORDAN

I'm always here. If I were not here, there'd be no here here. The detention hall would cease to exist if I were not given detention several times a week. *(Pauses)* The faculty in this school doesn't get my humor. Apparently, I come off as difficult and challenging to authority.

AVERY

That's too bad. A good sense of humor is an important quality to have.

JORDAN

You'd think. But wit like mine is wasted in the eighth grade. My counselor says it doesn't pay to be subversive in middle school.

(The washroom door slams open. AVERY jumps in surprise, scurries closer to JORDAN.)

TAYLOR

(enters, snarling over a shoulder): If you don't cut that out, I'll squash you like a bug.

(No response from DEVON, who enters immediately behind TAYLOR, wearing earbuds and playing air guitar.)

TAYLOR

DID YOU HEAR ME?

(DEVON looks up from the guitar, smiles at TAYLOR, not noticing the aggressive face, pumps both fists in the air like a rock star, wanders upstage, and then continues playing.)

TAYLOR

I wish Devon was playing an actual guitar. Then at least I could smash it in a million pieces.

MASON

(entering the room behind TAYLOR and DEVON): Some people have no appreciation for the musical arts. It's sad. Hey, Jordan. *(notices AVERY)* Hi, we haven't met— I'm Mason. I like the stuffed cat.

(AVERY tries to shove the cat back in the bag again.)

JORDAN

(to MASON): You're not supposed to see it.

MASON

(waves off AVERY's discomfort): That's cool. I got you covered on the not-seeing-the-cat deal. Very metaphysical; I like it. Have you met Taylor and Devon yet?

JORDAN

(to AVERY): Taylor's hostile and Devon's mellow so they make a nice matched set. An ideally balanced subset of the collection of people to be stuck in the bathroom during a storm with. *(JORDAN and MASON nod knowingly at each other. AVERY looks back and forth between TAYLOR, who's glaring at DEVON, and DEVON, who's playing so hard the strumming arm is windmilling. AVERY starts anxiously twisting the cat's ears, which are poking out of the bag.)*

JORDAN

Devon's the best musician in school. The only problem

is Dev's never so much as touched a real guitar. But look at that showmanship! A forward-thinking entrepreneur would send that act on the road, charge a modest admission at small clubs. Who knows? Maybe even work Dev up to an international major stadium tour gig, opening for world renowned rock gods.

MASON

Your faith in Devon has always been very touching, Jordy.

TAYLOR

It's your fault Devon's still wandering around like this, Jordan; you encourage bad behavior to take the focus off of yourself.

MASON

Taylor, that was uncharacteristically aware of you. A little mean, but good eye: Jordan, no offense, does throw others under the bus to avoid the consequences of having a smart mouth and an all-around disrespectful attitude.

(Before JORDAN can respond, the door flies open again.)

REGAN

Can you believe we're stuck in the john because of a little rain? Coach canceled practice because of *(exaggerating)* *drizzle* and a *light breeze. (notices DEVON flailing around on air guitar)* Santana? *(MASON and JORDAN nod, TAYLOR snorts and turns away. AVERY keeps nervously twisting the cat's ears.)* Better than pretending to be Hendrix, pretending to set the pretend ax on fire. *(Holds up a flat palm in a don't-go-there gesture)* Now that's crazy. Speaking of crazy, what's with the kid petting the stuffed cat in the bag?

MASON

That's Avery. First day here. Seems a little more anxious than crazy.

JORDAN

And we're not supposed to call attention to the cat. It's the exact opposite of Devon's guitar.

MASON

Which we're not supposed to *see* so much as *hear*.

JORDAN

There's a lot of existential reality in this school.

REGAN

I'm okay with that non-cat and the non-guitar. *(REGAN looks back and forth between AVERY and TAYLOR. Everyone nods agreeably, except TAYLOR who looks back and from DEVON to AVERY, sneering.)* Maybe we can get a picture for the yearbook of Avery and Devon and the nonentities; as editor-in-chief this year, I'm freaking out about how to fill up all the pages. I'll take anything. Even pictures of invisible felines and imaginary stringed instruments.

TAYLOR

Everyone in this school except me is nuts.

MASON

And yet you're the only one in this room failing. C'mon, Taylor, get your books out, let's finish that book report so we can be one step closer to being free of each other once and for all.

REGAN

(to AVERY): Mason is tutoring Taylor.

JORDAN

Taylor's resisting. If Mason were a germ and Taylor was an open wound, Taylor would be studied by the worldwide medical community as the future hope of preventing the spread of infectious disease.

REGAN

(still explaining to AVERY, who's looking back and forth between REGAN and JORDAN as they share the explanation, and studying TAYLOR and MASON who are sitting together sharing a book): Mason's only working with Taylor to get

a recommendation from the principal to attend the mock congress in Boston this summer.

JORDAN

They can't stand each other. Two people who loathe each other more do not exist in this world or any universe known to mankind or yet to be discovered. It's awesome entertainment for the rest of us that they have to work together. We've placed bets on how long it'll take one to smack the other with a thesaurus, and who'll take the first swing.

REGAN

Our school policy is zero tolerance for bullying so, if I should personally witness such behavior, in my role as student body president, I'd have to report it. Was it *report it* or *step in?* Hmm, can't remember.

MASON

(*throws head all the way back in very put upon gesture, speaks to the ceiling in frustration)*: Taylor's failing English. Our mother tongue. My whole future depends on teaching someone the difference between *I-T-S* and *I-T-apostrophe-S*.

TAYLOR

(glares at MASON and then turns and explains to AVERY): I'm not failing. I'm just not passing by as much as I should be. *(turns back to MASON in frustration)* And you said "it" was an imprecise and meaningless word that takes up space and should be avoided as much as possible. So what's the big difference if there's an apostrophe or not if I'm not supposed to use the word in the first place? Geez.

MASON

(sighs and hands TAYLOR a book, pointing to a page): Focus.

SOUND CUE #2: LOUDSPEAKER ANNOUNCEMENT: This is a weather update: The severe weather alert for the county immediately adjacent to ours is in effect until four thirty p.m. We are advised that strong winds are moving westward and that occasional rain or thundershowers are forecast with possible street flooding in low-lying areas. Total rainfall amounts are projected to vary between one to two inches.

JORDAN

Isn't that like, a miniscule amount of precipitation that's hardly even noticeable? I swear, this school is the drama queen of the entire district—always making a big deal out of nothing. It's not like anyone just reported seeing animals walking two by two to get on a big boat; it's not that kind of storm.

REGAN

Better safe than sorry. I hope they let us out soon, though; I've got to get over to the senior center by dinnertime because I'm volunteering today. Speaking of dinner: I'm starving. Anyone got anything to eat?

JORDAN

You're going to eat in the bathroom? Next to a stall? Eww.

REGAN

It's not like I was planning to suck water out of the toilet.

(JORDAN tosses REGAN a baggie of trail mix/raisins pulled from a backpack. They start aiming pieces at each other's open mouths like seals at the zoo. DEVON hurls himself on the floor.)

AVERY

(a little panicky): Devon is lying down on the floor. Why is Devon lying down on the floor like that?

JORDAN, REGAN, MASON, and TAYLOR

(as one answer): Acoustic set.

JORDAN

Devon's resting while the lead vocalist takes the spotlight; it's only for one song. *(DEVON jumps up, starts playing again)* See!

AVERY

(relieved): Oh. Okay.

(JORDAN and REGAN are eating, MASON and TAYLOR are studying, DEVON is playing air guitar in the corner. AVERY looks around the room, starting to get uneasy.)

AVERY

So, that's it? We're stuck in the bathroom?

JORDAN

(nodding): Yup.

AVERY

For who-knows-how-long?

JORDAN

Looks that way.

REGAN

Pull up some floor, relax.

AVERY

And none of you are worried about the storm?

JORDAN

This school is known for overreacting about bad weather.
Someone sees one teeny tiny bolt of lightning in the sky
and the whole place is on lockdown. It's nothing.

MASON

Yeah, if it was really bad, they'd be telling us to hide
under desks and cover our heads. Like that time last
year, remember? *(Everyone except AVERY and DEVON
nod)* This is sooooo not a big deal. The teachers haven't
even checked on us.

REGAN

(bored voice): The weather cell will pass by and then

someone will get on the loudspeaker and announce we're free to go. I give the whole containment thing another twenty, thirty minutes tops.

AVERY

I have to call my parents; they don't know where I am. No one knows where I am.

JORDAN

That's not entirely true; WE know where you are.

REGAN

Besides, you're fourteen years old—your folks aren't gonna freak out about where you are at four o'clock in the afternoon on a school day.

AVERY

My parents freak out if I lock the bathroom door when I take a shower. *(reacts to their surprised faces)* What if I slip on a bar of soap, hit my head, get knocked unconscious, land in the water that collects at the bottom of the tub after my forehead bumps the drain thing shut and then drown because they can't get to me fast enough because they're having trouble trying to unlock the door with a Phillips head screwdriver?

JORDAN

And they think that's a likely scenario?

AVERY

My parents have heard of stranger things happening.

TAYLOR

Your parents are neurotic. *(turns to MASON)* Hah! Neurotic: Vocab word.

MASON

Now spell it.

TAYLOR

You're a buzzkill. I used it correctly in a sentence. And I keep telling you: I don't need to know how to spell.

MASON

Yes, you do. We've gone over this before. Spellcheck on your computer is not the same thing as knowing how to spell.

(AVERY starts pacing, tugging at collar, running hands through hair.)

REGAN

(to AVERY): You okay?

AVERY

Not really. Is it just me or does this room seem to be running out of, I don't know, oxygen?

JORDAN

Highly unlikely. *(takes deep breath)* Yep, oxygen levels seem fine to me. Look at my hands: My fingertips and nailbeds are nice and pink, which means my O2 saturation is good.

REGAN

(to AVERY): Are you getting claustrophobic? Do confined spaces make you uncomfortable?

AVERY

Not as much as the lack of air. Can we open a window?

TAYLOR

During a storm? *(shakes head in disgust)* And people think I'm the dumb one.

JORDAN

No one thinks you're dumb. We think you're disagreeable. Maybe even a little abusive.

MASON

(protesting): I think Taylor might be dumb. I think we can't entirely rule out that possibility.

REGAN

(to AVERY, who is starting to pant): Sit down and put your head between your knees, breathe deep and slow. We'll all just breathe together, calmly. No one's going to panic or run out of air. *(speaking slowly and carefully, like a hypnotist putting someone under, getting the others to start breathing together too)* It's allllllllllll goooooooooood. Verrrrrry comforting and laaaaid baaaaaaack.

(AVERY, JORDAN, MASON, REGAN, and TAYLOR quietly breathe, synching their breaths, soothing AVERY down together; the room is silent.)

DEVON

ROCK AND ROLL! *(DEVON suddenly starts snapping*

fingers and head-bobbing, twirling in a funky shuffle-slide across the floor, head back, complete abandon.)

(AVERY squeaks and jumps in surprise at DEVON'S unexpected bellow.)

JORDAN

Thanks, Dev, way to add to the tranquil atmosphere.

(DEVON can't hear JORDAN but fist-pumps and dances in circles as if to agree.)

REGAN

Hey, I know. Let's take our minds off being trapped in the bathroom. Taylor, put the book down and come over here. Wanna be like King Tut? *(starts wrapping Taylor in toilet paper like a mummy. REGAN tosses AVERY a roll.)* Here. Make a mummy cat. The ancient Egyptians used to bury their pets with them, so it's historically valid, plus you'll feel better with something to do.

(MASON and JORDAN start tossing toilet paper rolls at each other, like two-person juggling, keeping three in the air at all times. AVERY's wrapping the cat in toilet paper and starting to smile, breathing has regulated.)

AVERY

Thanks. I do feel a little better.

MASON

Sure you do. Always good to keep your hands busy. Takes your mind off your worries.

JORDAN

So does talking. Let's play "would you rather?"! Mason, would you rather have a job cleaning up after a kangaroo with loose bowels or live in a sweaty giant's work boots?

MASON

I would rather not play "would you rather." Regan, poke an airhole in the toilet paper so Taylor can breathe. I'm pretty sure someone like Taylor doesn't have any brain cells to spare.

JORDAN

Okay, then, how about "guess who it is by the smell of their armpits"?

REGAN

No fair, I just ran laps before the weather got bad. I stink like fetid death.

JORDAN

(sniffing) Good point. How about "truth or dare?" Truth: What's the most embarrassing thing you've ever done?

AVERY

Brought a stuffed cat to school on my first day.

MASON

Well, since you mentioned it: What's the deal?

AVERY

Oh, uh, well, my, uh, my little brother must have, uh, hidden it in my bag this morning. Just snuck it right in there without me even noticing. Because I was worried about the new school.

REGAN

That was thoughtful. Has it helped?

AVERY

If you consider sleeping through the whole day helping, then, yeah, huge assist.

JORDAN

Again, since you brought it up, why'd you sleep all day?

AVERY

I only meant to nap through science. They were dissecting fetal pigs.

REGAN

Squeamish?

AVERY

No. Vegan. I'm not down with animal rights violation. I don't ingest, wear, or partake in the use of animals. *(lifts foot)* Even my shoes are made of canvas and hemp and contain no animal products, by-products, or derivatives.

JORDAN

Why?

AVERY

Because well-planned vegan diets have been found to offer protection against many degenerative conditions, including heart disease.

JORDAN

And that's a legitimate concern for a kid in middle school?

AVERY

My parents have heard of weirder things happening.

TAYLOR

(*from behind a mask of toilet paper*): Mmmumph gurrrrble dunderschmickzen.

MASON

Yeah, what Taylor said: How did "science class" become "all day long?"

AVERY

Once you've gone to sleep at school and missed a class or two—or five—it's kind of hard to find the correct reentry point. Every time I woke up, I worried about calling attention to myself by showing up late to class. So I just rolled over and went back to sleep.

JORDAN

Timing *is* everything. A good entrance is essential when

you're attempting to make a strong first impression. I'm feelin' you.

AVERY

Devon's lying down on the floor again. Another acoustic set?

JORDAN, REGAN, and MASON

(*as one*): Intermission.

AVERY

Sure, I should have guessed. (*Devon leaps up, starts playing again; Avery, sounding like an announcer:*) Annnnnnnnnnnnnd welcome to the second half of the show.

SOUND CUE #3: LOUDSPEAKER ANNOUNCEMENT: Occasional gusts of wind are moving west at nearly three miles per hour. They pose no immediate threat to this area. In the interest of the safety of the population of this school, however, please remain where you are. Until we are assured that all danger has passed, do not emerge from your safe location in an interior room, away from windows and flying objects.

(Everyone, except TAYLOR, who is still wrapped in toilet paper, picks up the nearest roll of toilet paper and hurls it at TAYLOR.)

JORDAN

I'm sure they meant dangerous flying objects.

TAYLOR

(ripping the toilet paper away from face and taking a deep breath): What stinks in here?

REGAN

Probably me. I repeat: Just came off the track after running laps.

JORDAN

It might be that we're in a restroom and you don't actually smell anything so much as the environment is highly suggestive to the existence of a malodorous scent.

TAYLOR

(looks confused): Hunh?

MASON

Jordy means you're imagining things, Taylor. I don't smell anything *(takes deep breath for emphasis)*. Oh, wait, scratch that: I *do* smell something funky.

(Everyone sniffs. Looks at each other suspiciously. Edges away from the stalls. TAYLOR peers in trash can.)

JORDAN

It's puke.

TAYLOR

Nah, it's toe jam.

REGAN

Nope. Limburger cheese.

MASON

You're all wrong: it's goat pee and used cat litter and fresh skunk and rotten chicken.

AVERY

(looks around, does a double-take, and tentatively sniffs the mummy cat. He looks embarrassed and shoves the cat back in the duffel bag): Uh, actually it's the stuffed cat.

TAYLOR

Your stuffed cat?

MASON

No, Taylor, the stuffed cat that the builders put in the

air vents for good luck and to drive away bad spirits. How many stuffed cats do you imagine we're dealing with here? Today? In this restroom?

TAYLOR

Is that a trick question? Like that Venn diagram thingie you tried to show me? Are there somehow three cats in circles and there's an overlap of the stinky and the non-stinky and the possibly stinky cats I'm supposed to figure out?

JORDAN

One cat, Tay.

TAYLOR

I knew it! I was right! I'm not always wrong, no matter what Mason says.

REGAN

Why does your cat stink like death, Avery?

AVERY

It's not my cat; it's my brother's cat, he's only four. Four-year-olds have stuffed cats. It's perfectly normal. For a four-year-old. But I have no idea why it reeks like this. It doesn't normally smell like vomit.

JORDAN

Apparently, confined spaces combined with the warmth of your head resting on the bag all day adversely altered the chemical compound of whatever the stuffed cat was originally stuffed with, turning it into a rancid stink bomb. There are some extra credit science points in there some-where if you figure out the hows and the whys of the mys-tery stench. I'm just saying—you might need some bonus projects to submit, seeing as how you cut class today.

(DEVON switches from air guitar to a combination of air drums and air piano, twisting back in forth slamming the drum heads and pounding the keyboards. DEVON holds up both hands, ring and middle fingers tucked under the thumbs,

index and small fingers up in the rock-and-roll sign, twirling
in circles and head-banging to a beat no one else can hear.
Everyone's head starts nodding in time. Eventually, DEVON
moves away from the keyboard and drum kit and starts playing
the guitar again, solo over.)

JORDAN

Don't take this the wrong way, but does anyone ever
wonder if there's something not quite right with Devon?

REGAN

You mean because of the way Dev doesn't seem to live in
the same world as the rest of us?

JORDAN

(nods): I love Dev—what's not to love about Dev, right?—
and it's not like Devon hasn't been like this since kindergarten and we've all gotten used to things but, you
know, looking at the situation with fresh eyes, a person
starts to wonder.

MASON

What I wonder is why Devon's even at school this late anyway. Taylor and I were in the library, studying; Regan was at practice and Jordy was in detention because that's where Regan and Jordan always are; and Avery was asleep—but does anyone know why Devon was still roaming the halls playing guitar so long after school was dismissed?

TAYLOR

Devon missed the bus. And I don't mean just today. *(looks at Mason and smirks)* It's a metaphor.

MASON

Spell it. And if you use an *F*, I'll throw my shoe at you.

REGAN

It doesn't take a third-year psych student to figure out Dev's the teeniest, tiniest bit touched in the head, as my great-aunt Blanche would say.

AVERY

We haven't actually spoken—Devon *can* hold a conversation, right? *(everyone shrugs)* But I get the feeling Devon's a good person. I like people who are different.

JORDAN

Then you are in the right middle school restroom with the right five people. Because, not to brag or anything, but you could not have set out to gather together a group of people who are more unhinged than us.

REGAN

Speak for yourself. I am the very definition of the clean-cut all-American scholar-athlete young citizen role model. The fact that I am wickedly good-looking and heart-meltingly charming is a happy bonus.

MASON

(to AVERY): Regan took more than one person's share while standing in the self-confidence line. *(REGAN nods,*

tries to look humble; MASON continues): My only problem is that I might be too smart to fit in with my peers.

TAYLOR

Mason took more than one person's share while standing in the ego line. *(turning to MASON)* And you spell that *C-O-N-C—E I-*before-*E-*except-after-*C T-E-D. (MASON applauds)* The only problem I have is a low tolerance for goofballs. Which, if you ask me, is pretty much everyone in this school.

AVERY

None of you are anything like the kids from my last school.

JORDAN

What was that like?

AVERY

It wasn't a school so much as a—now don't overreact to the word—but *commune.*

JORDAN

You're going to have to do some explaining.

AVERY

Commune might be the wrong word. *(pauses)* A bunch of parents and their kids lived together as one big family, raising a garden for food and sharing all the responsibilities.

JORDAN

Commune is the exact right word.

AVERY

We only lived there for a few months. Just to see what it was like. My folks like to try new things.

MASON

Have you tried out any other alternative lifestyles we should know about? Other than that vegan thing you talked about before?

TAYLOR

Like living in a tree house, maybe doing without electricity or prime numbers?

MASON

Taylor, I'm impressed. I don't believe you can actually *name* a prime number, but big props for knowing the phrase. We'll circle back to that concept later. *(MASON and TAYLOR high-five)*

REGAN

I could totally live off the land if I had to live in a commune. Hunting, fishing, building shelter.

JORDAN

You could not. You were worried about starving to death during a storm emergency.

REGAN

That's because I was surprised and didn't have time to

get all my gear together. Under normal circumstances, I'm known for my preparedness. Gotta be on top of things when you're in as many activities as I am.

JORDAN

I can't believe we haven't voted you CEO of the school yet.

REGAN

Me too! CEO, COO, CFO, and whatever other C-Os there are. I *am* the personification of school spirit in this building.

JORDAN

That's the kind of thing you generally let other people say; announcing it just makes you come off even more obnoxious than you already are.

REGAN

I know. But I don't let things like that get me down. I'm

awesome that way. I am the most perfectly well-adjusted person you'll ever meet. Probably because I'm in a ton of activities and have more friends than anyone else.

JORDAN

You say that like they're good things.

REGAN

I say that like it's the secret to life. Which, by the way, it is.

MASON

I think you're wrong, Regan, the secret to life is good grades and enrichment classes and advanced placement and extra credit. For a person like me. But, Jordan, if I were you, I'd listen to what Regan has to say.

REGAN

Thanks, Mason, we'll get back to you in a second. But first, semirhetorical question: Anyone notice that Jordan gets nosebleeds a lot?

JORDAN

(defensive, gingerly touching nose): Yeah? So what.

REGAN

I read that bloody noses can be a side effect of nerves.

JORDAN

I'm the least nervous person you'll ever meet, Regan. I'm an extrovert, in case you hadn't noticed. Class clown. Most likely to make people pee from laughing at my jokes.

REGAN

You refused to try out for the school play when I asked you to keep me company at auditions.

JORDAN

I found the play selection derivative and trite.

REGAN

You had a completely bogus excuse for why you couldn't
be my partner on the debate team.

JORDAN

What's bogus about the fact that it was a Thursday of a
full moon week and my horoscope warned me to avoid
oral conflict?

REGAN

You said you didn't have time to devote to being in the
big buddy program with me at the elementary school.

JORDAN

That would have entailed afternoon meetings and, as you
know, I've got a standing date with the detention hall.

REGAN

You've never tried out for a single team, even though I
always invite you to go out for basketball, tennis, track,

soccer, lacrosse, and golf when I'm being evaluated for
the teams.

JORDAN

What's your point?

REGAN

My point is that I think you might be insecure.

JORDAN

(snorts): I'm just not into calling attention to myself.
Unlike Devon. *(DEVON is now leading a clap-along, arms
overhead, clapping to a steady beat, as if rousing the crowd to
get to their feet and join in)*

REGAN

Devon commits to the moment.

JORDAN

Yeah, too bad Devon doesn't commit to reality. *(winces,*

slaps forehead and shakes head in disgust. Everyone nods understandingly.)

REGAN

If I were to bet, I'd say that you secretly wish you were more like Devon. Go on, stand there and look me in the eye and tell me you don't dream of becoming a stand-up comedian. I'd put money on the fact that you practice one-liners in the bathroom mirror and take notes so you'll have funny things to say in conversations, don't you?

(JORDAN shifts uncomfortably, can't think of anything to say.)

AVERY

I think Regan makes a good point about you and Devon: One of you is living the dream; the other one has deten-tion all the time and a lot of bloody noses. *(They turn and study DEVON who is rocking the neck of the guitar up*

and down, arching back as if in a backbend and then leaning
forward in a crouch and prowling across the stage, bent over,
knees bent, totally blissed out.)

JORDAN

(sighs and throws up hands in defeat): Okay, you got me.
Clearly, we should all be more like Devon and Regan.

REGAN

(hands JORDAN a piece of paper): Here. You can get over
your fear of speaking doing a set at the fundraiser next
week. You'll tell jokes for a good cause and overcome
your performance anxiety by playing to a crowd bigger
than one.

JORDAN

(signs paper and hands it back): So, I'm going to join at
least one of Regan's extracurricular activities. Good
thing it's the one that plays to my skill set: I'll be able
to wander around telling random jokes, maybe even

doing a few improv skits. *(wheels around as if facing a live audience and points)*: "You! Come up here on the stage next to me. An escaped convict, the grease trap of an Atlantic City casino's kitchen stovetop, and a misunderstanding about a blind date. Now improvise a scene with me using those ideas and . . . GO!"

AVERY

I actually think that sounds kind of amazing. I'll sign up and get involved if you will—probably easier if we have each other's backs. I'll be less likely to doze through another school day if I know someone's got my back around here.

JORDAN

You don't have a little brother, do you?

AVERY

No.

JORDAN

The stuffed cat belongs to you, doesn't it?

AVERY

Yeah. But not the puke smell. I don't know where *that*
came from.

REGAN

Backstage. You do not even want to know what happened after the musical last month. Thought we'd
cleaned everything up. Guess not.

JORDAN

Now that we all know the stuffed cat belongs to you, are
you going to leave him at home?

AVERY

Probably just get a bigger bag.

JORDAN

That's what I figured.

REGAN

I love when stuff works out so I look like the really cool person with all the answers. *(pauses to reflect)* It happens a lot, but it never gets old.

MASON

That's very chummy for you three and, no doubt, in the best interests of the entire school. But Taylor and I have a book report to finish. Taylor, you have one last paragraph to write and then you're done. Then, today, when your mother asks you what you did today, you can say, "Spared Mason from dying of frustration and boredom by finishing my homework assignment." She'll be so proud.

REGAN

What about you, Mase? What are you going to tell your mom about what you and your friends did today?

MASON

She would never ask that. Because she knows that I don't have friends. I have well-connected contacts. And influential references. And helpful associates. And challenging academic colleagues.

TAYLOR

Nah. That's not all. You have friends.

MASON

Right. You want me to believe that you actually stopped to think about whether or not I have a big enough social circle?

TAYLOR

(clears throat and very carefully recites the following list): Two, three, five, seven, eleven, thirteen, seventeen, nineteen, and twenty-three.

AVERY

Cool! First Devon tunes out and has a little concert going on in the corner. Then Jordan turns into a human punch-line generator. Now Taylor's become a number-spewing savant. You cannot tell me there isn't something really unique in the air at this school. Even my parents would not believe weirder things could happen.

MASON

(smiles, confused, impressed, uncertain): No. That's not it; those are prime numbers. Taylor just listed prime numbers. *(facing TAYLOR)* You *have* been paying attention when we work together.

TAYLOR

Not only is it hard to tune someone like you out, but *(clears throat and takes a deep breath)* concomitant with your mistaken belief that I'm not nearly as bright as you are, is the insulting way you have ignored the fact that I am ideal friend material.

AVERY

What did Taylor just say?

REGAN

Is that still Taylor?

JORDAN

Shhhhh. I want to hear Taylor explain why it was a good idea to play dumb just to cozy up to Mason.

MASON

You pretended to be stupid so I'd tutor you?

TAYLOR

Don't flatter yourself; I was struggling—a bit—to catch up after I had mono last term and I needed some help. For a while. A *little* while. But then I kind of liked hanging out with you; you're not so bad for an antisocial intellectual snob who doesn't have time for amigos.

MASON

You have a weird way about you.

TAYLOR

Anyone can make a friend the old-fashioned way, "hey, we have a lot in common and get along, wanna hang out and watch TV?" Boring. My way showed . . .

MASON

(jumps in and finishes the sentence with TAYLOR): Panache.

SOUND CUE #4: LOUDSPEAKER ANNOUNCEMENT: Attention! The storm warnings have been lifted for this entire area. The weather is clear and it is now safe to leave your secure area. Thank you for your cooperation.

DEVON

(steps forward and comes all the way downstage, facing the audience, slips the air guitar strap off, holds it high in the air, and takes a huge bow): Thank you. Thank you very much.

We hope you enjoyed our music. The band and I had a blast. You're a great audience. Rock on! We love you. See you next time. Drive home safely! Good night!

CURTAIN FALLS